MOONBEAM
AND THE BIG JUMP

SELMA AND JACK
WASSERMANN

ILLUSTRATIONS
GEORGE ROHRER

BENEFIC PRESS
WESTCHESTER, ILLINOIS

The Moonbeam Books

Library of Congress
Number 68-56126

Copyright 1969 by Benefic Press
All Rights Reserved
Printed in the United States of America

Contents

The Plane

Moonbeam works at the Rocket Port.

She is a chimp.

Scott works with Moonbeam.

He likes Moonbeam.

"Look out, Moonbeam!" said Scott.

Something was coming fast.

It was a plane.

Moonbeam jumped!

The plane looked big.

"Hoon! Hoon!" said Moonbeam.
She wanted to be in the plane.
She liked to go fast.
"Soon," said Scott and laughed. "You
will soon go up in a plane."

"You will go up," Scott said. "And you will jump out."

Moonbeam looked at Scott.

"Heeeeeen!" she said.

Scott laughed.

"It will be a slow jump," he said.

"You will jump with a parachute."

Moonbeam liked to jump.

She wanted to jump now.

Up she jumped.

And down she came — in the water.

"Heen! Heen!" she said.

Moonbeam did NOT like water.

"Look at you," said Scott. "Now you will have to have a bath."

"Heen!" said Moonbeam. "Heeeen!"

"Come on," said Scott.

Moonbeam went with Scott.

Soon they saw Dr. Jim.

Dr. Jim saw Moonbeam and laughed.

"One chimp bath coming up!" he said.

"Heen!" Moonbeam said again.

And what a bath it was!

When Moonbeam was out of her bath,
Dr. Jim looked at Scott.

"What now?" he said.

"Moonbeam has to find out what
parachute jumping is," said Scott.

"Come on, then," said Dr. Jim.

Moonbeam went with the two men.

Barney Hopper

"Here we are," said Scott.

"Hoon!" said Moonbeam.

She went in with Scott and Dr. Jim.

FRONT BACK

CHUTE

ROPES

MAN

"Look, Moonbeam," said Dr. Jim.

"That is what a parachute looks like."

Moonbeam looked at the parachute.

"Where is Barney Hopper?" said Scott.

"He helps Moonbeam with her jumping."

"Here he is now," Dr. Jim said.

Barney Hopper came in.

Moonbeam looked at Barney.

He was big!

"Come here, chimp," said Barney.

"Come on! Here we go!"

"See that plane, chimp?" Barney
Hopper said.

Moonbeam looked.

She saw the plane.

She saw men in it, too.

One of the men in the plane was not
a parachute jumper.

He looked at the other men.

The men looked at him.

Then he said, "JUMP!"

The men jumped.

And Moonbeam jumped!

Up she went.

And down she came.

And the water came down on Moonbeam!

"Heeeeen!" said Moonbeam.
Scott and Dr. Jim laughed.

Barney Hopper looked at Moonbeam.
"You see, chimp?" he said. "When you
jump, you have to look where you are
going. Now, look at the jumpers."

19

Moonbeam looked.
She saw one of
the jumpers jump
out of the plane.
Down and down he fell.
Faster and faster he fell.
"Heen! Heen!" said Moonbeam.

Then Moonbeam saw the jumper pull
something in the parachute.

She saw the parachute open.

The parachute worked.

It slowed the jumper down.

"Hoon! Hoon!" said Moonbeam.

Soon the jumper was down.

"Have a good look, chimp," said
Barney. "You will have to come down
like that."

"Hoon! Hoon!" said Moonbeam.

Water! Water!

"Come on, chimp," said Barney Hopper.
"Come on, men."

Moonbeam, Scott, and Dr. Jim went
out with him.

"Up you go,"
said Barney.
Moonbeam went up.
"Now jump down,"
said Barney.
"Hoon! Heeen!"
said Moonbeam.
Then she jumped.
Down she came.

"Not like that, chimp," said Barney.

"On here!"

"Hon? Hon?" said Moonbeam.

"Up you go again," said Barney.

Up went Moonbeam.

"Jump!" said Barney.

Down jumped Moonbeam.

"That looked good," said Scott.

"I liked that jump," said Dr. Jim.

Barney Hopper did not look at the two men. He looked at Moonbeam.

"Again!" Barney said.

Again and again
Moonbeam went up.
Again and again
she jumped.
Again and again
Barney looked at
her come down.

Then Barney said, "That is it for now, chimp. We will work again soon."

"Hoon! Hoon!" said Moonbeam.

She went with Scott.

"You can stop jumping now,
Moonbeam," said Scott.

Moonbeam liked to jump.

She did not want to stop.

She wanted to go on jumping.

Up went Moonbeam.

And down she jumped.

She jumped and jumped.

"Stop!" said Scott.

Moonbeam did not stop.

Up she went again.

Down came Moonbeam — in water!

"Heeeeen!" she said. "Heen! Heen!"
Scott laughed.

"You did not want to stop,
Moonbeam," he said. "Now you will
have to have a bath again."

"Heeeeen!" said Moonbeam.

A Parachute for Moonbeam

Moonbeam did not like her bath.
"Heen! Heen!" she said.

Then Scott came with something.

"Look, Moonbeam," he said. "I have
something for you."

"Hon? Hon?" said Moonbeam.

"This is a parachute," said Scott.
"A parachute for you."

"Hoon! Hoon!" said Moonbeam.

"We will soon have it on you,"
said Dr. Jim.

Scott looked at Moonbeam with her
parachute on.

"That looks good," he said. "Now
come on. Barney Hopper is looking for
you. This jump will be a big one!"

"Hoon! Hoon!" said Moonbeam.

"Here it is," said Scott.

"What a jump this will be!" said
Dr. Jim.

Moonbeam looked up.

"Hoon!" she said. "Hoon! Hoon!"

Then Barney Hopper came.

"Here we go, chimp," he said.

"You go up with
Moonbeam, Scott,"
said Dr. Jim. "I
will be here when
she comes down."

Moonbeam went
up with Barney
and Scott. Up and
up they went.

Then they came to a stop.

Moonbeam and Scott looked down.

"Hoon! Hoon!" said Moonbeam.

"Oooof!" said Scott. "Moonbeam has
to jump down there?"

"The chimp can jump it," said Barney.
"You will see."

"I can not look," said Scott.

"Do you see this, chimp?" said Barney.
"When you jump, pull it."

"Hon? Hon?" said Moonbeam.

"Jump and pull, chimp," said Barney.
"Jump and pull."

Moonbeam did not look at Barney.
She wanted to jump now.

Barney looked at Moonbeam.

"Jump!" he said.

Moonbeam jumped.

"Pull!" said Barney.

Moonbeam did not pull.

Her parachute did not open.

"Pull! Pull!" said Barney and Scott.

Moonbeam did not pull.

Faster and faster she fell!

Then the two men did not see her!

"Moonbeam!"
said Scott.

Scott went fast.
Down, down,
down he went.

Barney Hopper
came down, too.

The two men went
faster and faster.

Then Scott stopped.

"Moonbeam!" he said.

"Heeeeeen!" said Moonbeam.

She was in water again!

"Heen! Heeeeen!" she said.

Scott laughed.

And the other men laughed, too.

Up, Up, Up

"Do you see that, chimp?" said Barney. "You will have to pull. Jump and pull!"

"What now?" said Dr. Jim.

"Up we go again," said Barney.

They all went up again.

Again they came to a stop.

"Will she pull on this jump?" said
Scott. "Will she? Will she pull to
open her parachute?"

"The chimp will pull," said Barney.

He looked at Moonbeam.

"Jump!" said Barney.

Moonbeam jumped.

Down and down
Moonbeam fell.

Then she pulled!
Her parachute
opened up.

"Hoon! Hoon!"
said Moonbeam.

She came down.

Scott and Barney and Dr. Jim looked down at Moonbeam.

"That looked like a good jump," said Scott. "What now?"

"Now the chimp will come up here," said Barney. "And she will jump again and again."

Moonbeam worked at her jumping.

Again and again she went up.

Again and again she jumped.

Again and again she pulled, and her parachute came open.

Then Barney looked at Moonbeam.
"That will be all for now. See you
soon, chimp," he said.

Here We Go!

"Come on," said Barney Hopper. "Up, chimp. Up! Up!"

Moonbeam jumped up.

Scott jumped up.

"What? Where?" said Scott.

"To work again," said Barney. "To work, chimp."

"Here it is," said Barney. "You will jump out of this plane, chimp."

"Hoon! Hoon!" said Moonbeam.

Moonbeam and Scott and Barney went to the plane.

"In you go, chimp," said Barney.

Moonbeam jumped in.

Scott went with Moonbeam and Barney.

Scott looked at Moonbeam.

"What a big jump this will be, Moonbeam," Scott said.

"Hoon! Hoon!" said Moonbeam.

Then the plane went.

Faster and faster it went.

And then the plane went up!

Up, up, up it went.

"Hoon! Hoon!" said Moonbeam.

Scott laughed.

"Moonbeam likes this plane," he said.

Pull! Pull!

"Come and look down," said Barney.

"I can see the Rocket Port," said
Scott. "And look at all that water."

Moonbeam wanted to see.

She came to have a look.

"Look out,
Moonbeam! Look
out!" said Scott.

"You can not jump
here, chimp," said
Barney. "Look out!"

Moonbeam did not
look at the two men.

She looked down.

Then the plane
did something.

"Hon? Hon, hon?"
said Moonbeam.
And out she fell!

"Pull!" said Scott.
"Pull on it."
"Pull, chimp!
Pull!" said Barney.
Moonbeam looked
up at the two men.
What did they
want?
Moonbeam fell
and fell and fell.

Then it came to her.

The parachute!

Moonbeam pulled on it.

Then the parachute opened and slowed Moonbeam down.

"Hoon! Hoon!" said Moonbeam.

She liked this parachute jump.

Down and down she went.

And then Moonbeam came to a stop.
She was in water again.

"Heeeeeeen!" she said.

Where Moonbeam looked, all she saw
was water, water, water.

"Heeeeeen! Heeeeeen!" she said.

She wanted help.

Moonbeam did not see help coming.

She looked up and down.

Then she did see something.

It was a boat!

It was coming to help her.

Moonbeam saw a boy on the boat.

And she saw his father.

"Here, I will help you up,"
said the boy.

Soon Moonbeam was in the boat.

"A chimp? With a parachute?" said
the boy. "What is going on?"

"This chimp must be from the Rocket
Port," said the father. "We will soon
find out."

"Come in, Rocket Port! Come in!"
said the father. "We have a chimp with
a parachute here. Is it yours?"

Then something said, "This is Rocket
Port. The chimp is Moonbeam."

"We are coming," said the father.
"You will soon have your chimp."

The boat went on.

Moonbeam and the boy wanted to see where it was going.

"Look!" said the boy. "The Rocket Port!"

"Hoon! Hoon!" said Moonbeam.

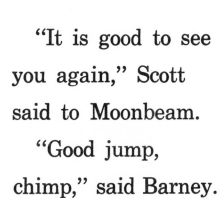

"It is good to see
you again," Scott
said to Moonbeam.

"Good jump,
chimp," said Barney.

"But look at you!"
said Dr. Jim. "You
will have to have a
bath again!"

"Heeeen! Hoon!"
said Moonbeam.
The men laughed.

"Look at that chimp
go," they said.

Vocabulary

The total vocabulary of this book is 96 words, excluding proper names and sound words. The 33 words in roman type should be familiar to children reading on a primer level. The 16 words above primer level are shown in italic type. The number indicates the page on which the word first appears.

again 11
all 49
at 5

bath 10
be 7
boat 59
boy 60
but 63

came 9
chimp 5
coming 6

do 39

fast 6
faster 20
fell 20
from 60

going 19

has 12
helps 14
her 12
him 17
his 60

jumper 17
jumping 12

laughed 7
looking 35

men 12
must 60

now 9

of 12
open 21
other 17
out 6

parachute 8
plane 5
pull 21

slow 8
Something 6
Soon 7
stop 29

That 14
then 12
there 38
two 12

was 6
water 9
When 12
works 5

yours 61

Edited by
Joellen Reiter